D1053209

# DISNEY
# ENCANTO
## THE GRAPHIC NOVEL

Random House 🏠 New York

rhcbooks.com

ISBN 978-0-7364-4284-8 (trade) — ISBN 978-0-7364-4285-5 (ebook)

Printed in the United States of America
10 9 8 7 6 5 4 3

# DISNEY
# ENCANTO

## THE GRAPHIC NOVEL

Random House 🏠 New York

# meet the
# MADRIGALS

Hidden in the mountains of Colombia is an enchanted place, an Encanto, where the Madrigal family lives. In their vibrant town, the Madrigals have a magical house they call Casita. It helps the members of the family out. Casita's like another member of the household! Even more miraculously, the Encanto has blessed everyone in the family with a unique gift, ranging from superstrength to the power to heal. It blessed everyone except . . .

# Mirabel

Mirabel is a bright, charismatic, funny, and sensitive young woman who has grown up, as the only Madrigal without a gift, trying to measure up to her family's talents. When she discovers that the magic of the Encanto is in danger, she sees the perfect opportunity to prove her worth and show her family her true value. Mirabel loves her family and would do anything for them.

# meet the
# MADRIGALS

## Abuela Alma

Abuela Alma is the family matriarch, whose deep love produced a miracle for her family in their darkest hour. She is mother to the triplets Julieta, Pepa, and Bruno. She is strong and is determined to do whatever is necessary to protect her family. Though some might feel Abuela Alma's need for perfection is too much, she's not one to let the concerns of others get in the way of doing what she believes is right. But underneath her tough facade, Abuela Alma is deeply worried for the future of her family and the Encanto.

## Abuelo Pedro

Abuelo Pedro was Alma's husband and the patriarch of the family. He died fifty years ago, when he and Abuela Alma left their home in search of a better life. Abuela Alma attributes the miracle of the Madrigal family to his sacrifice.

# Agustín

Agustín is Julieta's husband and the father of Mirabel, Luisa, and Isabela. Though his city upbringing makes him seem like a fish out of water in the town, he's a funny, loving, and supportive father and husband. He doesn't have a magical gift since he married into the family, but he does play the piano.

# Julieta

Julieta is the mother of Mirabel, Luisa, and Isabela. She is warm, kind, and creative, and she has the gift of healing people's ailments through the delicious food she makes. She worries about Mirabel, but she is always open and supportive when her daughter needs her.

# Isabela

Isabela is Mirabel's oldest sister. The perfect golden child of the family, her gift is the ability to make beautiful flowers bloom anywhere. She moves with effortless grace and poise, like a princess who never had to practice. She's more complex than she appears, however, and she secretly feels trapped by the need to be perfect.

# Luisa

Luisa is Mirabel's other older sister. She is extraordinarily athletic and gifted with superstrength. She's strong enough to lift two donkeys or even an entire building! Luisa is truly the rock of the family— she's tough and funny, though, deep down, she wonders if she would be of value without her strength.

# meet the
# MADRIGALS

## Bruno

One of the triplets, Bruno is Pepa and Julieta's estranged brother. As a child, he was the family's shining star due to his ability to see the future. Over time, the family began to believe that Bruno's visions led to bad consequences, so he shut himself off from the family and the rest of the world.

# Pepa

Pepa is the mother of Dolores, Camilo, and Antonio. She is energetic and funny. She is also very emotional, which can sometimes be an issue since her gift is the ability to alter the weather based on her emotions!

Felix is Pepa's husband and father to Dolores, Camilo, and Antonio. He is kind and is always the life of the party. Felix loves his wife very much and wants nothing more than to make her happy.

# Felix

# meet the
# MADRIGALS

## Dolores

Born shortly after her perfect cousin, Isabela, Dolores has spent her life in Isabela's shadow. Gifted with superhuman hearing, Dolores learns a lot of secrets and can't wait to share them.

# Camilo

Mirabel's cousin Camilo has the ability to transform his appearance. He uses his amazing gift to help people in the town—whether they need someone really tall or really short, Camilo can do it all.

# meet the
# MADRIGALS

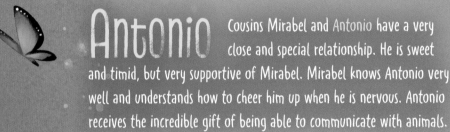

## Antonio

Cousins Mirabel and Antonio have a very close and special relationship. He is sweet and timid, but very supportive of Mirabel. Mirabel knows Antonio very well and understands how to cheer him up when he is nervous. Antonio receives the incredible gift of being able to communicate with animals.

WHAT'S YOUR GIFT?

WELL, IF I ONLY TELL YOU *MY* PART, YOU WON'T KNOW THE WHOLE STORY.

WHAT'S THE WHOLE STORY?

DID YOU HEAR THEM, CASITA? *LET'S GO!*

WELCOME TO THE *FAMILY MADRIGAL.* THIS IS OUR HOME!

Moments later, la Casa Madrigal and everyone in the family are using their special gifts to decorate for Antonio's ceremony.

MY BABY'S NIGHT HAS TO BE PERFECT. ANTONIO'S NIGHT IS GOING TO BE A DISASTER. I CAN'T BELIEVE THIS!

AMOR, YOU'RE TORNADOING THE FLOWERS!

DID SOMEONE SAY "FLOWERS"?

Everyone but Mirabel.

WOW. MIRA, YOU OKAY? YOU DON'T HAVE TO OVERDO IT.

I KNOW, MAMÁ. I JUST WANT TO DO MY PART. YIKES! BEESTINGS!

FIRST GIFT CEREMONY SINCE YOURS, LOTS OF EMOTIONS. WHEN YOUR TÍO FELIX AND I MARRIED INTO THE FAMILY— OUTSIDERS WHO HAD NO GIFT, WE...

PEPA, THE SKY HAS A CLOUD.

I KNOW, MAMÁ. I CAN'T FIND ANTONIO.

OOH, I BET I CAN FIND HIM!

NO, I'M SURE YOU NEED TO GO GET CLEANED UP.

IT'S NO PROBLEM. ANYTHING I CAN DO TO HELP.

MIRABEL, I KNOW YOU WANT TO HELP. BUT TONIGHT...MUST BE PERFECT.

THE WHOLE TOWN RELIES ON OUR FAMILY, ON OUR GIFTS.

SO THE BEST WAY TO HELP IS...TO STEP ASIDE, LET THE REST OF THE FAMILY DO WHAT THEY DO BEST. OKAY?

EVERYONE'S LOOKING FOR YOU.

THIS PRESENT WILL SELF-DESTRUCT IF YOU DON'T TAKE IT IN THREE, TWO, ONE...

NERVOUS? YOU HAVE NOTHING TO WORRY ABOUT. YOU'RE GONNA GET YOUR GIFT AND OPEN THAT DOOR. IT'S GONNA BE THE COOLEST EVER!

WHAT IF IT DOESN'T WORK?

WELL...IN THAT IMPOSSIBLE SCENARIO...YOU'D STAY HERE IN THE NURSERY WITH ME. FOREVER.

I KNOW YOU ARE AN ANIMAL GUY.

I MADE THIS SO YOU ALWAYS HAVE SOMETHING TO SNUGGLE WITH IN YOUR NEW ROOM.

ALL RIGHT, HOMBRECITO. READY?

Guests are arriving at Casa Madrigal for Antonio's gift day celebration.

THERE YOU ARE. READY FOR THE BIG SHOW?

ABUELA SAYS IT'S TIME!

FIFTY YEARS AGO, THIS CANDLE BLESSED US WITH A MIRACLE.

TONIGHT, WE COME TOGETHER ONCE MORE AS ANOTHER STEPS INTO THE LIGHT... TO MAKE US PROUD.

Mirabel is reminded of her ceremony ten years ago...

but she summons the strength for Antonio.

I CAN'T...

I NEED YOU.

COME ON. LET'S GET YOU TO YOUR DOOR.

Every step is a painful reminder...

of the worst night of her life.

GASP!

WILL YOU USE YOUR GIFT TO SERVE THIS COMMUNITY AND MAKE US PROUD?

SQUAWK

UH-HUH, I UNDERSTAND YOU!

WE HAVE A NEW GIFT!

As the family comes together, Mirabel begins to feel separate...

I KNEW YOU COULD DO IT! A GIFT JUST AS SPECIAL AS YOU!

!

and less worthy.

WE NEED A PICTURE, EVERYONE! COME, COME!

IT'S A PERFECT NIGHT!

EVERYONE SAY...

"LA FAMILIA MADRIGAL!"

POOF!

Then, as the others start celebrating...

I'M NOT FEELING SAD.

AFTER ALL, I'M STILL PART OF THE FAMILY. I'M FINE.

NO, I'M NOT FINE! I'D LOVE TO SHINE LIKE ALL OF THEM!

I'M READY FOR A CHANGE. I WANT TO HEAL WHAT'S BROKEN AND SHOW THIS FAMILY WHAT I CAN DO! BUT I'M TIRED OF WAITING ON A MIRACLE.

IS IT TOO LATE FOR A MIRACLE?

CRACK!

~GASP!~

OUCH!

HUH?

VRRRRR

CASITA? ARE YOU... OKAY?

CRACK

CASITA?

CRACK CRACK CRACK

CRAAAACK

Later, as the party continues, Mirabel joins Julieta in the kitchen.

IF IT WAS ALL IN MY HEAD, HOW DID I CUT MY HAND? I WOULD NEVER RUIN ANTONIO'S NIGHT. IS THAT REALLY WHAT YOU THINK?

I THINK THAT TODAY WAS VERY HARD FOR YOU—

I WISH YOU COULD SEE YOURSELF THE WAY I DO. YOU ARE JUST AS SPECIAL AS ANYONE ELSE IN THIS FAMILY.

I WAS LOOKING OUT FOR THE FAMILY. AND I MIGHT NOT BE PERFECT LIKE ISABELA, BUT... WHATEVER...

MM-HMM. YOU JUST HEALED MY HAND WITH AN *AREPA CON QUESO*.

I HEALED YOUR HAND WITH MY LOVE FOR MY DAUGHTER, WITH HER WONDERFUL BRAIN, HER BIG HEART...

AGH!

SMOOCH

MAMÁ!

I KNOW WHAT I SAW.

MIRA, MY BROTHER BRUNO LOST HIS WAY IN THIS FAMILY... I DON'T WANT THE SAME FOR YOU.

Later, everyone goes out to help the community, and…

LUISA? WHAT'S GOING ON? WHAT ARE YOU HIDING?

NOTHING. JUST GOT A LOTTA CHORES, SO MAYBE YOU SHOULD GO HOME.

TELL ME WHAT YOU KNOW... LUISA? YOU'RE OBVIOUSLY NERVOUS ABOUT SOMETHING— IS IT ABOUT LAST NIGHT?

I'M THE STRONG ONE. I'M NOT NERVOUS.

THUD

But suddenly, Luisa opens up to her sister for the very first time.

I KEEP HELPING EVERYONE, AND I'M NOT ALLOWED TO MAKE MISTAKES. I'M ALWAYS UNDER PRESSURE.

HUH? I THINK YOU REALLY NEED A BREAK.

LUISA DOESN'T TAKE BREAKS. YOU WANNA FIND A SECRET ABOUT THE MAGIC...GO TO BRUNO'S TOWER, FIND HIS LAST VISION.

VISION OF WHAT?

NO ONE KNOWS. THEY NEVER FOUND IT.

WAIT! HOW DO YOU EVEN "FIND" A VISION?

IF YOU FIND IT, YOU'LL KNOW. BUT BE CAREFUL...THAT PLACE IS OFF-LIMITS FOR A REASON.

There's no time to waste, so Mirabel gathers her courage, and...

CAN YOU TURN OFF THE SAND? CASITA?

WHOOOSH

YOU CAN'T HELP IN HERE.

I'LL BE FINE. I NEED TO DO THIS. FOR YOU. FOR ABUELA...MAYBE A LITTLE FOR ME.

FIND THE VISION. SAVE THE MIR— ACK!

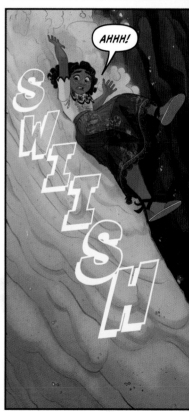

AHHH!

SWIISH

MIRABEL, WHERE ARE YOU COMING FROM IN SUCH A HURRY?

UH... I'M SORRY... I WAS, UM...

I'M LOSING MY GIFT! AFTER OUR LITTLE TALK, I REALIZED I WAS BEHIND.

WHEN I WENT TO GRAB THE DONKEYS, THEY WERE...HEAVY!

DID YOU SAY SOMETHING TO HER?

UH... I JUST...

DING DONG

THE GUZMÁNS ARE EXPECTING ME IN TOWN! TELL NO ONE. THERE'S NOTHING WRONG WITH LUISA, AND WE CAN'T HAVE THE FAMILY IN A PANIC. TONIGHT IS TOO IMPORTANT.

Moments later...

WHY AM I IN YOUR VISION, BRUNO?

ROARRR CRASH

TÍA, JEEZ!

I JUST WANTED TO GET THE LAST OF ANTONIO'S THINGS, AND THEN I HEARD "THE NAME WE DO NOT SPEAK"!

TÍA PEPA— IF HE HAD A VISION ABOUT SOMEONE, WHAT DID IT MEAN FOR THEM?

WE NEVER TALK ABOUT BRUNO!

HE WOULD SEE SOMETHING TERRIBLE AND THEN CRACK- BOOM, IT WOULD HAPPEN!

"IT WAS THE DAY OF OUR WEDDING..."

"THE SKY WAS PURE BLUE..."

IT'S GOING TO RAIN...

CRACK-BOOM

"BRUNO'S WORDS GOT INTO PEPA'S MIND, AND..."

ON THE DAY OF OUR WEDDING... A HURRICANE!

THERE'S NO TALKING ABOUT BRUNO.

I WISH I HADN'T ASKED ABOUT HIM.

When everyone leaves Mirabel's room, just as the Guzmáns are about to arrive...

NO...

MIRABOO! GOT YOUR PARTY PANTS ON? CAUSE I DO—

≈GASP!≈

I FOUND BRUNO'S LAST VISION. THE MAGIC IS DYING. I THINK IT'S ALL BECAUSE OF ME!

WE SAY NOTHING. ABUELA WANTS TONIGHT TO BE PERFECT.

JUST ACT NORMAL. NO ONE HAS TO KNOW.

But...

HUH!

MIÉRCOLES!

UH...ISABELA, MOST GRACEFUL OF ALL THE MADRIGALS...

YOU'RE DOING GREAT!

WILL YOU... MARRY ME?

CRACK

CRACK

WHAT IS *HAPPENING?*

MIRABEL FOUND BRUNO'S VISION!

SHE'S IN IT! SHE'S GONNA DESTROY THE MAGIC!

As the cracks start spreading, everyone's powers fritz and spasm....

WHOOSH

CRACK

THUD

CRACK

AHH! MY NOSE!

COME, MARIANO! I'VE SEEN ENOUGH! WE'RE LEAVING!

WAIT! PLEASE! SEÑORA, *POR FAVOR!*

I HATE YOU!

I'M A LOSER!

WHAT DID YOU DO?

I'M NOT DOING ANYTHING! IT'S BRUNO'S VISION! IT'S...

BRUNO ISN'T HERE!

I KNOW THAT... I KNOW HE ISN'T...

HERE.

SQUEAK

SQUEAK

Following the rats, Mirabel finds...

HUH?

SWISH

CREAK

a secret passageway!

Mirabel enters the passageway within the walls and...

=GASP!=

STOP!

STOP!

SWISH

NO, NO— HELP! CASITA! HELP ME!

TÍO BRUNO! WHY DID YOU TAKE THE VISION? HOW LONG HAVE YOU BEEN BACK HERE?

EVERYTHING WAS PERFECT!

ABUELA WAS HAPPY. THE FAMILY WAS HAPPY.

APOLOGIZE FO RUINING MY LIF OUT! GO!

WAIT! ISA, FINE, I *APOLOGIZE*. I'M SORRY...THAT YOUR LIF IS SO PERFECT! YOU SELFISH PRINCESS!

ISA, I KNOW WE'VE... HAD OUR ISSUES... BUT I'M READY... TO BE A BETTER SISTER. SO WE SHOULD JUST... HUG IT OUT.

*HUG* IT OUT? LUISA CAN'T LIFT AN EMPANADA. MARIANO'S NOSE LOOKS LIKE A SMASHED PAPAYA. HAVE YOU LOST YOUR MIND?

SELFISH? I'VE BEEN STUCK BEING PERFECT MY ENTIRE LIFE.

NOTHING IS MESSED UP! YOU CAN STILL MARRY THE BIG DUMB HUNK—

THE ONLY THING YOU'VE EVER DONE FOR ME IS MESS THINGS UP!

I NEVER WANTED TO MARRY MARIANO. I WAS DOING IT FOR THE FAMILY!

ISA...?

POP

WHAT DID YOU DO?

I JUST MADE SOMETHING NEW!

IT'S NOT PERFECT, BUT IT'S...MINE!

I WONDER IF I CAN DO MORE?

HUG

THERE'S NOTHING YOU CAN'T DO!

I'LL NEVER BE GOOD ENOUGH FOR YOU, NO MATTER HOW HARD I TRY.

NO MATTER HOW HARD *ANY* OF US TRIES. LUISA WILL NEVER BE STRONG ENOUGH.

ISABELA WON'T BE PERFECT ENOUGH. BRUNO LEFT OUR FAMILY BECAUSE YOU ONLY SAW THE WORST IN HIM—

BRUNO DIDN'T CARE ABOUT HIS FAMILY.

HE LOVES THIS FAMILY. *I* LOVE THIS FAMILY.

WE ALL LOVE THIS FAMILY.

YOU'RE THE ONE BREAKING OUR HOME!

DON'T YOU EVER!

*CRACK*

*CRACK*

THE MIRACLE IS DYING BECAUSE OF YOU!

Suddenly, the whole Encanto shakes...

*CRAAAAAAAACK*

NO, NO, NO, THE CANDLE!

MIRABEL...

I'M SORRY. I DIDN'T WANT TO...HURT US... I JUST WANTED TO BE SOMETHING I'M NOT.

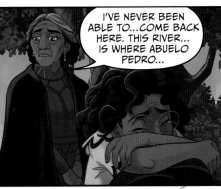

I'VE NEVER BEEN ABLE TO...COME BACK HERE. THIS RIVER... IS WHERE ABUELO PEDRO...

But when Abuela looks into the water...

I THOUGHT WE WOULD HAVE A DIFFERENT LIFE... I THOUGHT I WOULD BE A DIFFERENT WOMAN.

Mirabel sees how Abuela and Abuelo met...

⇒GASP!⇐

and fell in love.

SHE DIDN'T DO THIS! I GAVE HER A VISION. I WAS LIKE, GO!

AND SHE WAS LIKE, FTTT! SHE ONLY WANTED TO HELP!

I...DON'T CARE WHAT YOU THINK OF ME, BUT IF YOU'RE TOO STUBBORN TO—

BRUNITO

I FEEL LIKE I MISSED SOMETHING IMPORTANT. WHERE ARE WE GOING?

HOME!

Later, in the Encanto...

MIRABEL...

MAMÁ...

AY, MI AMOR, I WAS SO WORRIED.

MAMÁ... WE'RE GOING TO BE OKAY.

Gift or no gift,
I am just as special
as the rest of my family.
—Mirabel

There's nothing you can't do!
−Mirabel

## GRAPHIC NOVEL

### SCRIPT ADAPTATION
Tea Orsi

### LAYOUT
Giovanni Rigano

### PENCIL & INK
Marco Forcelloni,
Rosa La Barbera,
Mario Oscar Gabriele,
Michela Cacciatore,
Elisa Cristantielli

### COLOR
Massimo Rocca,
Luigi Aimé,
Vita Efremova,
Nicola Righi,
Alla Khatkevich

### LETTERS
Chris Dickey

## COVER

### LAYOUT / PENCIL / INK
Marco Ghiglione

### COLOR
Cristina Toniolo

## DISNEY PUBLISHING WORLDWI
Global Magazines, Comics, and Partwork

### PUBLISHER
Lynn Waggoner

### EXECUTIVE EDITOR
Carlotta Quattrocolo

### EDITORIAL TEAM
Bianca Coletti (Director, Magazines),
Guido Frazzini (Director, Comics),
Stefano Ambrosio (Executive Editor),
Camilla Vedove (Senior Manager,
Editorial Development),
Behnoosh Khalili (Senior Editor),
Julie Dorris (Senior Editor),
Mina Riazi (Assistant Editor),
Gabriela Capasso (Assistant Editor)

### DESIGN
Enrico Soave (Senior Designer)

### ART
Ken Shue (VP, Global Art),
Roberto Santillo (Creative Director),
Manny Mederos (Senior Illustration
Manager),
Marco Ghiglione (Creative Manager),
Stefano Attardi (Illustration Manager)

### PORTFOLIO MANAGEMENT
Olivia Ciancarelli (Director)

### BUSINESS & MARKETING
Mariantonietta Galla
(Senior Manager, Franchise),
Virpi Korhonen (Editorial Manager)

### GRAPHIC DESIGN
Chris Dickey

### SPECIAL THANKS
Yvett Merino, Charise Castro Smith,
Lorelay Bove, Ian Gooding, Ashley Lam,
Stephanie Lopez Morfin, Heather Blodget
Kaliko Hurley, Angela D'Anna,
Alison Giordano, Jackson Kaplan,
Jeff Clark, Andrew Elmers